DISNEP
Winnie the Pooh

It's Fun to Learn

A Sense of Fun

It was apple-picking time in the Hundred-Acre Wood, and Rabbit's friends were helping him with the apple harvest.

The air was filled with the happy sound of friends laughing and the sweet smell of wood smoke drifting from Rabbit's chimney. And as far as the eye could see, there were apples. Red apples. Green apples. Yellow apples.

Owl sighed happily. "This is indeed a feast for the senses."

"A what for the whatses?" Tigger asked.

"What Owl means is that there are so many splendid things to see...and hear...and smell...and touch...and taste," said Christopher Robin, counting off the five senses on five fingers.

"Look around, Tigger," said Owl. "What do you see?"

Tigger looked around. "I see Long Ears upside down in a basket."

"And what do you hear?" Owl asked.

"I hear him yelling something that sounds a lot like 'HELP!'" Tigger said.

Just then, Rabbit peeked out from under the apple basket.

"I was wondering where you were, Rabbit," Piglet said. "Look!"

Rabbit saw Pooh picking the last apple in the orchard.

"We're finally done!" Rabbit cried. "And thank you, too," Rabbit added.

"I couldn't have done it without all of you."

"Didn't someone mention a feast?" Pooh asked hopefully.

"That's it!" Christopher Robin said. "We can have a feast for the senses. We can each make something good to taste or touch or smell or hear or see. And then we can share it with everyone else."

"I know what I'm going to make!" Roo said. "Rabbit, may I please take something from your garden?"

"Anything you want," Rabbit said. "That goes for all of you."

Soon everyone took apples or pumpkins home to use for the feast.

Everyone, that is, except Tigger.

Tigger couldn't think of anything to make for the feast. In fact, Tigger still wasn't quite sure what all of this sense stuff was about.

"Maybe this will be more sensical to me if I find out what everyone else is making," Tigger said.

Very early the next morning, Tigger knocked on Rabbit's door.

"What are you doing here?" Rabbit asked. "The feast isn't until tomorrow."

"I just wanted to see what sort of sense-type thinga-ma-bobs everyone is making for the feast," Tigger said. "You're my first stop."

"I'm making my famous apple jelly," Rabbit said proudly, pointing at the huge, steaming pots on his stove. "It smells wonderful, it tastes wonderful...."

"But it looks kinda' compli-catered," Tigger said.

"Oh, yes," Rabbit agreed. "It took me years to learn how."

"I don't have years," Tigger sighed. "I only have until tomorrow."

From Rabbit's house, Tigger bounced over to Piglet's.

Tigger heard cheerful humming coming from the kitchen. He followed the sound and found Piglet baking apple-haycorn muffins.

"Here—taste one," Piglet said.

"It's delicerous!" Tigger said. "And tasty, too!"

Tigger went to Pooh's house next.

"What happened to you?" Tigger cried when he caught sight of a very gooey Pooh.

"I'm trying out different ways to make honey apples for the feast," Pooh said. "I've figured out how to make them taste yummy, but they all feel rather sticky-ish when you touch them."

When Tigger got to Owl's house, Owl was reading about making yummy-smelling candles.

"It says here that apples and cinnamon make a particularly pleasing smell," Owl muttered.

"I say, Tigger, what do you think?" Owl asked.

Tigger sneezed. "Smells swell," he said.

Just then, there was a loud noise outside. "Did you hear that?" Owl asked.

Tigger nodded. "Tiggers have very sense-itive ears, you know."

Tigger looked out and saw Eeyore, pulling a barrel.

"I'm going to make cider," Eeyore explained. "If the barrel doesn't leak. Which it probably will."

Tigger's last stop was Kanga and Roo's house.

Before he even got to their door, Tigger smelled something wonderful.

The closer he got, the stronger the smell got.

Tigger sniffed. "My nose knows that's apple pie!" he cried.

Kanga gave Tigger and Roo each a slice of pie. "Don't touch the pies over here, dears," she warned. "They're still hot."

After they ate, Roo showed Tigger the maracas he had made by filling Rabbit's gourds with beans. "Listen!" Roo said, shaking them. "Don't they sound neat?"

Tigger thought Roo's maracas were wonderful. In fact, he thought everyone's everythings were wonderful. If only he had something special for the feast, too!

Tigger closed his eyes and listened to Roo's maracas. He took a deep breath and smelled Kanga's pies.

Suddenly Tigger had an idea! He knew what he was going to do for the feast!
"T-T-F-N—ta-ta-for-now!" Tigger called to Kanga and Roo as he hurried off.
"And T-F-E—thanks for everything!"

On the day of the feast, everyone came to the orchard bright and early to get things ready.

"Look, Mama!" cried Roo. "Rabbit made a mountain of jelly!"

"Oh, and listen!" Roo added. "His table is making groaning sounds!"

Eeyore was busy from the moment he arrived, serving hot apple cider.

"I love the way a hot drink feels in my hands on a cool morning," Piglet said.

"It tastes yummy, too," Pooh said. "Sort of sweet and spicy."

"Perfect with a piece of pie," Owl said. "And a haycorn muffin."

Christopher Robin brought sour apple candy that made everyone's lips pucker.

"Isn't it amazing how many different things you can make from apples?" he said. "Things that taste sour; things that smell sweet; things that feel hot; and things that feel smooth!"

"Don't forget things that feel sticky," said Pooh, taking honey from his pot.

Roo played every song he knew on his maracas. He sniffed every candle until he found the perfect pine-scented one for Kanga. He tasted two of everything.

But something was missing.

"Hey!" Roo cried. "Where's Tigger?"

"Over here, Buddy Boy!" called Tigger. He was standing next to a mysterious sort of curtain.

"I wanted to surprise everyone," Tigger said, throwing open the curtain. "This is my USE YOUR SENSES game."

"Hooray!" shouted Roo. "How do you play?"

"I cover your eyes," Tigger said. "And you use your senses to guess what's in the jars."

Roo leaned over the first jar. "No sound," he said.

"Smells sweet, and—EWWWW!" Roo laughed. "Feels gooey!"

"You can taste it," Tigger said.

"It's honey!" Roo shouted.

Everyone took turns playing Tigger's game.

"Kanga's pie!" Owl said as soon as he sniffed one of the jars.

"Maracas!" Rabbit called out when he heard the sound from his jar.

"I really should taste this again before I guess," Pooh said, dipping into the red jar.

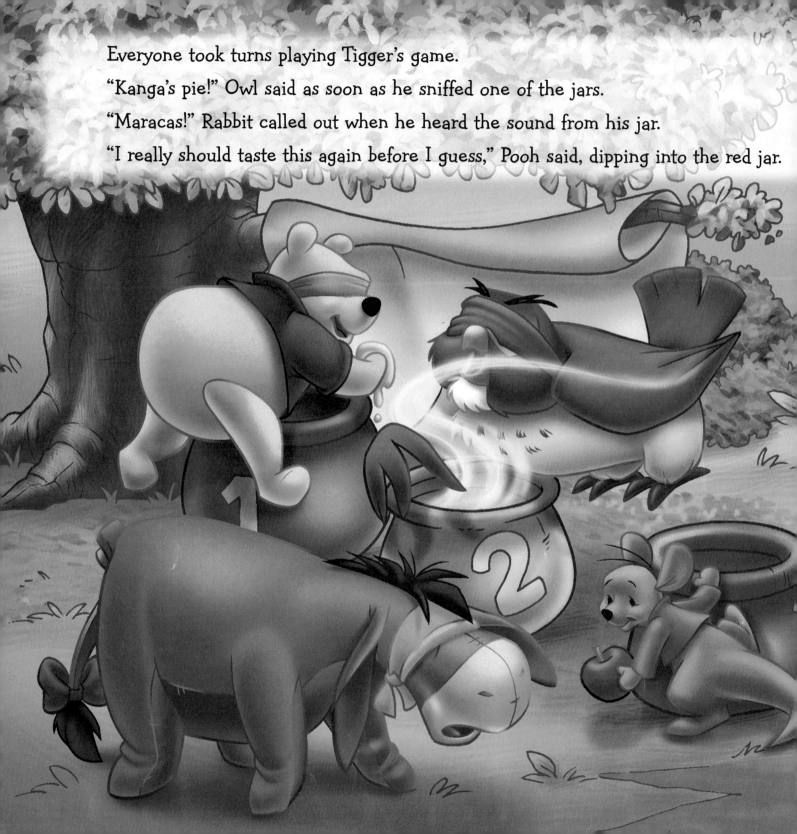

"This was a wonderful idea, dear," Kanga said to Tigger. "How did you think of it?"
"At first I couldn't think of anything sense-ational to do," Tigger said. "But then I remembered something important. I'm a tigger! And F-U-N is what tiggers do best!"

Fun to Learn Activity

Hoo-hoo-hoo! We had some sensational sense-type thingamabobs at our feast! Bounce back through the story and see how we used our senses: smell, touch, taste, sight, and hearing! Pooh-boy was busy tasting honey, but what about the rest of us? How did we use our senses?

Name the different ways you used your five senses today to smell, touch, taste, see, and hear the things around you.